EARLY BIRD STORIES™

Librarians in My Community

Gina Bellisario   Illustrated by **Ed Myer**

LERNER PUBLICATIONS ◆ MINNEAPOLIS

NOTE TO EDUCATORS

Find text recall questions at the end of each chapter. Critical-thinking and text feature questions are available on page 23. These help young readers learn to think critically about the topic by using the text, text features, and illustrations.

Lerner Publications Company
A division of Lerner Publishing Group, Inc.
241 First Avenue North
Minneapolis, MN 55401 USA

For reading levels and more information, look up this title at www.lernerbooks.com.

Photos on page 22 used with permission of: Tyler Olson/Shutterstock.com (librarian); Bloomicon/Shutterstock.com (device); wavebreakmedia/Shutterstock.com (young girl).

Main body text set in Billy Infant 22/28.
Typeface provided by SparkyType.

Library of Congress Cataloging-in-Publication Data

The Cataloging-in-Publication Data for *Librarians in My Community* is on file at the Library of Congress.
ISBN 978-1-5415-2021-9 (lib. bdg.)
ISBN 978-1-5415-2708-9 (pbk.)
ISBN 978-1-5415-2413-2 (eb pdf)

Manufactured in the United States of America
1-44357-34603-3/23/2018

TABLE OF CONTENTS

CHAPTER 1

THE SPY

Our class wants to find out what librarians do. We decide to visit Mr. Field, our school librarian.

"I'm an information expert," says Mr. Field. "What's something you really like?" "Dinosaurs!" says Joey.

Mr. Field searches for *T. rex* in his computer. Then he tells Joey where to find books about the *T. rex*.

Search: T. Rex

1. T. Rex Up Close
2. Incredible Dinos: T. Rex
3. How to Draw a T. Rex
4. T. Rex and Other Dinosaurs

Mr. Field says we can look for books about *anything* using the online catalog.

The catalog lists all the books and movies in our library. Mr. Field can also see things in other libraries.

Maybe Mr. Field is a spy.

How can you look up a book in a library?

9

CHAPTER 2

NO SHUSHING ALLOWED!

Jack is talking in the library.

"SHH!" whispers Grace.

But Mr. Field doesn't mind. He says making noise can help us learn. He plays music from around the world!

Speaking up is important for librarians.
It is how they share information.

They give library tours and puppet shows.

Librarians are full of facts.

Reading so much helps them know about all kinds of things.

How do librarians share information?

CHAPTER 3
A COMPUTER WIZARD

Our teacher Mrs. Ríos needs help. Her computer is stuck.

Mr. Field comes to the rescue!
He says librarians are technology wizards.

Mr. Field teaches us how to use computers for our schoolwork.

VIRUS
FREE

AREA

18

And he shows our teacher how to keep our computers safe from viruses.

Not every librarian works in a school. Some help out in museums or in hospitals.

Librarians also work at public libraries. These libraries are open to the community.

Mr. Field came to read us a story. We think he's a great helper!

Where else do librarians work besides schools?

LEARN ABOUT COMMUNITY HELPERS

Librarians are people in the community. A community is a group of people who live or work in the same city, town, or neighborhood.

Library books don't have to stay in the library. Students and teachers can check out books from the school library. Librarians use computers to keep track of what books are checked out.

A librarian named Melvil Dewey made finding books easy. He gave different numbers to different types of books. Librarians use the numbers to put the books in order. Many libraries use these numbers.

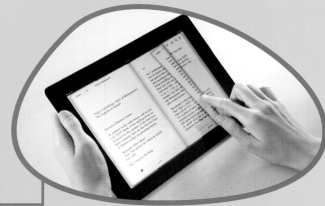

Many libraries have electronic books, also called e-books. You use a computer or other electronic reader to look at an e-book. Librarians can show you how they work. Librarians learn about new technology.

Most people study best in a quiet library. So many libraries have separate places for noisy learning. These are called play areas or story rooms.

THINK ABOUT COMMUNITY HELPERS:
CRITICAL-THINKING AND TEXT FEATURE QUESTIONS

How do you think librarians learn about new technology and other information?

Why do you think some people like to work quietly in a library?

Who is the author of this book?

Who created the artwork for this book?

GLOSSARY

catalog: a complete list of items, usually found on a computer, that can be borrowed from a library

electronic reader: a tool with which a person can read an e-book

technology: the tools people make to improve life. Technology in libraries includes bar codes and computers.

virus: a harmful program that stops a computer from working properly

TO LEARN MORE

BOOKS
Hopkins, Lee Bennett. *School People.* Illustrated by Ellen Shi. Honesdale, PA: WordSong, 2018. Read this book of poems about the people who work in a school, including librarians.

Rustad, Martha E. H. *Sam Visits the School Library.* Illustrated by Jess Golden. Minneapolis: Millbrook Press, 2018. Follow along with Sam as he visits his school's library and learns about what he can do there!

WEBSITE
It's Never Too Soon . . . to Start Thinking about a Career as a Librarian
http://www.ala.org/educationcareers/sites/ala.org.educationcareers/files/content/careers/librarycareerssite/children_flier.pdf
Visit the American Library Association website to see this fun flyer about a librarian's job.

INDEX